Saying Goodbye to Olivia

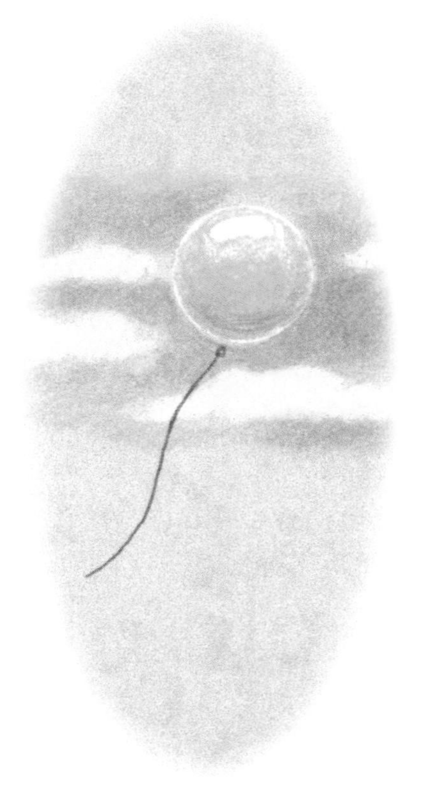

A Story of Loss and Hope

by Marie Kriedman

With Illustrations by Lawrence Goodridge

Saying Goodbye to Olivia

ISBN: 978-1-7359194-3-0

For information, contact the author:
Website: BooksbyMarie.com

Write Away K

Published by:

Chilidog Press LLC
pbronson@chilidogpress.com

Chilidog Press
Loveland, Ohio
www.chilidogpress.com

Illustrations by: Lawrence Goodridge
Cover by: Lawrence Goodridge
Design by: Craig Ramsdell

Dedication

For our beautiful, brave little girl.
Daddy and Mommy will love you forever.

Note from the Author

Dear reader,

I suffered a miscarriage unexpectedly at 14 weeks. My husband and I were at a complete loss. Setting aside my personal pain, the single hardest thing I had to do was tell our children about the miscarriage. I fumbled my words and halted and tried again, and finally managed to break the news.

I channeled that conversation, and many others that followed, into this book. If your family finds itself needing this book, perhaps you are going through something similar. I am so sorry for your loss, and I wish you peace as you heal.

Saying Goodbye to Olivia

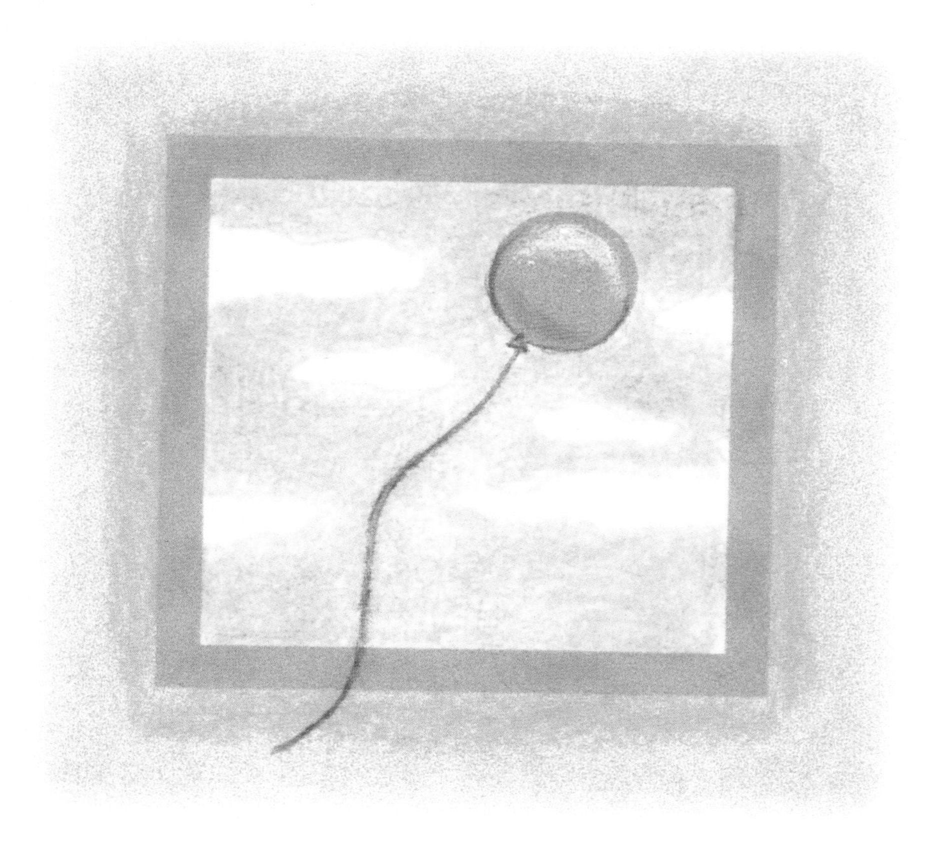

Have you ever had a day that starts normal but ends up very different? I had one of those too. I would like to tell you the story about that day.

It was a lazy Sunday. Those days are the best! My little brother and I were watching a movie when I noticed Mommy and Daddy were using loud voices. But they weren't fighting. And they were both crying. It was very unusual.

Mommy said she had to leave for a little while but she would be back. I felt confused about what was happening. When Mommy came home, she and Daddy said they had something important to tell us.

“Mommy was going to have a baby but the baby was sick and did not live,” she said. “That’s why Mommy was gone. I went to the hospital, so the doctors could help me have the baby.”

“How did the baby get in your belly without making a hole?” my brother asked.

Mommy smiled. “Mommy and Daddy made the baby,” she said.

“Was it a boy or a girl?” I asked.

"The baby was a girl and her name is Olivia," Mommy said.

"Why won't the baby be born?" I asked.

"When you have a baby too early, it is called a miscarriage," Mommy said. "The baby was born today but she was too little and she died. The baby was always safe because she was inside Mommy's tummy."

"Can I see the baby?" my brother asked.

"No, you can't see her," Mommy said. "But we can talk about her. Any time you have questions or want to talk about her, then let us know."

Daddy explained that Olivia was still a part of our family. "We are going to celebrate her birthday every year," he said.

"When is her birthday?" I asked.

"Today is her birthday," Daddy said. "August 16th."

"How will we have her birthday if she's not here?" I wanted to know.

“We are going to celebrate her every year because she is still a part of our lives,” Daddy said. “We will have a cake for her just like we do for you, and we will talk about her. There are lots of ways to remember someone who has died. We can plant a tree, send a balloon to heaven, volunteer, or do something special on Olivia’s birthday.”

Mommy started crying.

“Mommy and Daddy love Olivia very much, just like we love you very much,” Daddy said. “We are very sad that Olivia isn’t here, so you are going to see us cry sometimes. I know it’s scary when you see us crying, but it’s OK. We are going to be sad for a long time.”

"It's OK if you have a day where you are feeling sad too," Mommy said. "Tell Mommy and Daddy, and we can talk, and do lots of hugs and cuddles. There will also be days where you don't feel sad and that's OK too."

"Are we going to have another baby?" I wanted to know.

"I don't know," Mommy said. "We might have another baby or we might enjoy our family just the way it is."

"Where is the baby now?" my brother asked.

“Olivia is not alone,”
Mommy said.

"She is with Grandma and Grandpa, and Aunt Ethel. Do you remember them? They died too, and they are going to take care of her for us, and give her lots of hugs. And she is with our kitty cats that died. They are all together. That is how we know everything will be OK."

We talked for a long time and there were lots of things to think about. Mommy was right. Sometimes it was normal in our house, and sometimes Mommy or Daddy cried. I didn't like that.

When she was sad, Mommy would have quiet time alone in her room, and sometimes she and Daddy would hug for a long time. I liked to give hugs too. Mommy said it was a great idea!

"Your hugs always help me feel better," Mommy said.

A couple of days later, I had a question. "What can I do for Olivia?" I asked. "Can I volunteer on my own?"

"I know you're 6 and do lots of big-boy things, but you can't volunteer alone," Daddy said. "That is something we will do together as a family."

"But what can I do all by myself?" I asked.

"That is a great question," Mommy said. "You really like to draw. Would you like to make a special card to honor Olivia? We could send it to a friend or to someone who lives in a retirement community."

"Yes! I would like to do that," I said.

"Drawing a card will be a wonderful surprise to help brighten someone's day," Mommy said.

"What about me?" my little brother asked.

"Hmmm. That's a tough one," Daddy said. "I know you want to do something special too, but when you're 4 you still need lots of help."

"What about a game?" he asked. "Can I play a game to help remember Olivia?"

"What a good idea!" Mommy said. "Instead of playing a game, what if you pick a game or a toy or a book? We can give it to the school library or children's hospital, and then lots of boys and girls can have a turn."

"But I still want to play a game," he said.

"You got a deal," Mommy smiled. "You pick something to donate, and we will play a game together too."

"OK!" he said. "I like that."

"I like that too," Mommy said. "It hurts right now and we will be sad for a long time, but we will be OK. Olivia is with people who love her and she is watching over us. She will check on us from time to time, and we can let her know we are thinking about her when we celebrate her or talk about her."

"And we are OK. We love each other and we love Olivia, and we will get through this together. We will be OK."

Mommy was right. We got through that unusual day and all the rest… together. But we never forgot our sister. Olivia will always be a part of our family because she is in our hearts.

Resources for families

www.nationalshare.org

www.childrengrieve.org

www.dougy.org

www.compassionbooks.com

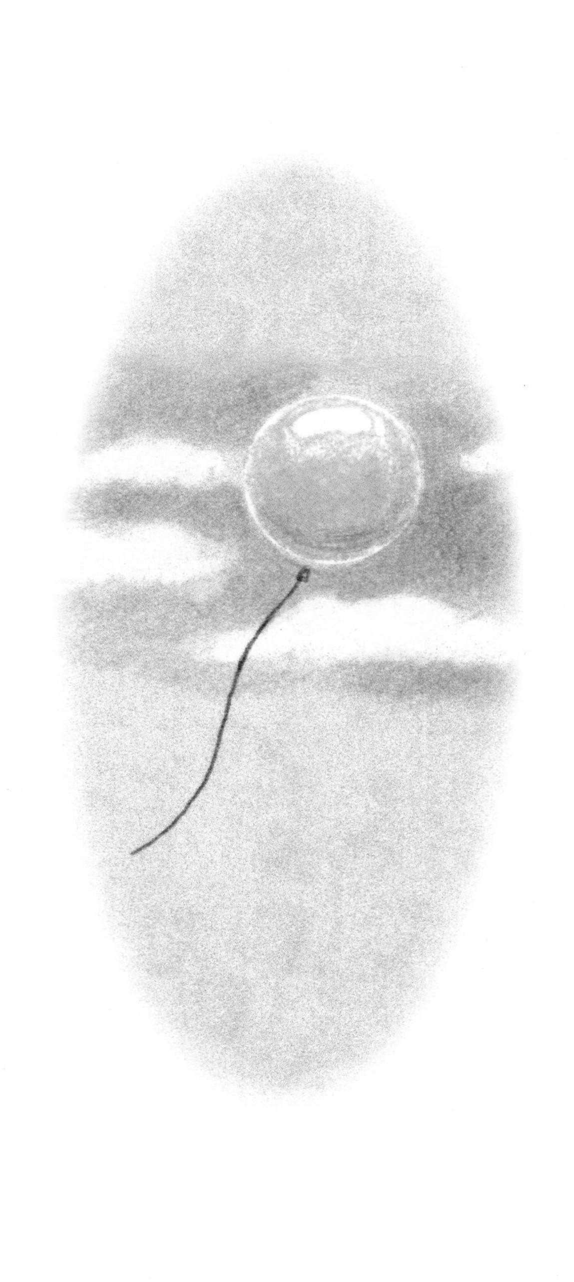